Are There Dinosaurs In Space?

Written By: Kristin Maggio & Sally Baldwin

Illustrated by: Kristin Maggio

www.kristinsartavenue.com

Copyright 2016 1st edition

Published by: Kristin's Art Avenue

ISBN: 978-0692666159

This book is dedicated to Veronica Federiconi, Dana Ranke, and Rachael Tremblay. You are some of the most inspiring women we have ever known. xo

When dinosaurs roamed the earth

They ruled the land and felt their worth

With lots of room to sway as they walked

Their tails went swoosh

They roared when they talked

Then people came and traffic was born

Cars and trucks and lots of horns

The dinosaurs needed so much more

To roam about like they did before

So they went into space, that was the key

Where their sway and swoosh could again be free

They roar all day when inspired

No one hears them, no silence required

They dine on moon dust and lots of stars

They dance on Jupiter and sleep on Mars

They play baseball with asteroids

Then swim in the deep dark craters

They jog on Venus and save tennis for later

They skate on Saturn's ring of ice

Mercury is for board games and rolling the dice

Uranus is the place for bowling

Pluto is nice for midnight strolling

But Neptune's where they love to stay

And practice all their swoosh and sway

Because they have so much space

They can line up to start a race

In the clouds they play hide and seek

I see their shapes when out they peek

So next time you hear the sound of thunder

I bet you will also sit and wonder....

Are there dinosaurs in space?

I do believe that is the case.

www.ingramcontent.com/pod-product-compliance
Lightning Source LLC
Chambersburg PA
CBHW041611120626
46551CB00002B/397